JAZZ SOLOS
Playalong *for* Tenor Saxophone

Wise Publications
part of The Music Sales Group
London/New York/Paris/Sydney/Copenhagen/Berlin/Madrid/Tokyo

Published by
Wise Publications
8/9 Frith Street, London W1D 3JB, England.

Exclusive Distributors:
Music Sales Limited
Distribution Centre, Newmarket Road, Bury St. Edmunds,
Suffolk IP33 3YB England.
Music Sales Pty Limited
120 Rothschild Avenue, Rosebery, NSW 2018, Australia.

Order No. AM979638
ISBN 1-84449-450-0
This book © Copyright 2004 by Wise Publications.

Compiled and edited by Christopher Hussey.
Music arranged by Simon Lesley.
Music processed by Camden Music.
Cover photography by George Taylor.
Printed in Great Britain.

Your Guarantee of Quality:
As publishers, we strive to produce every book to
the highest commercial standards.
The music has been freshly engraved and the book has been
carefully designed to minimise awkward page turns and
to make playing from it a real pleasure.
Particular care has been given to specifying acid-free, neutral-sized
paper made from pulps which have not been elemental chlorine bleached.
This pulp is from farmed sustainable forests and was
produced with special regard for the environment.
Throughout, the printing and binding have been planned to
ensure a sturdy, attractive publication which should give years of enjoyment.
If your copy fails to meet our high standards,
please inform us and we will gladly replace it.

www.musicsales.com

Saxophone Fingering Chart

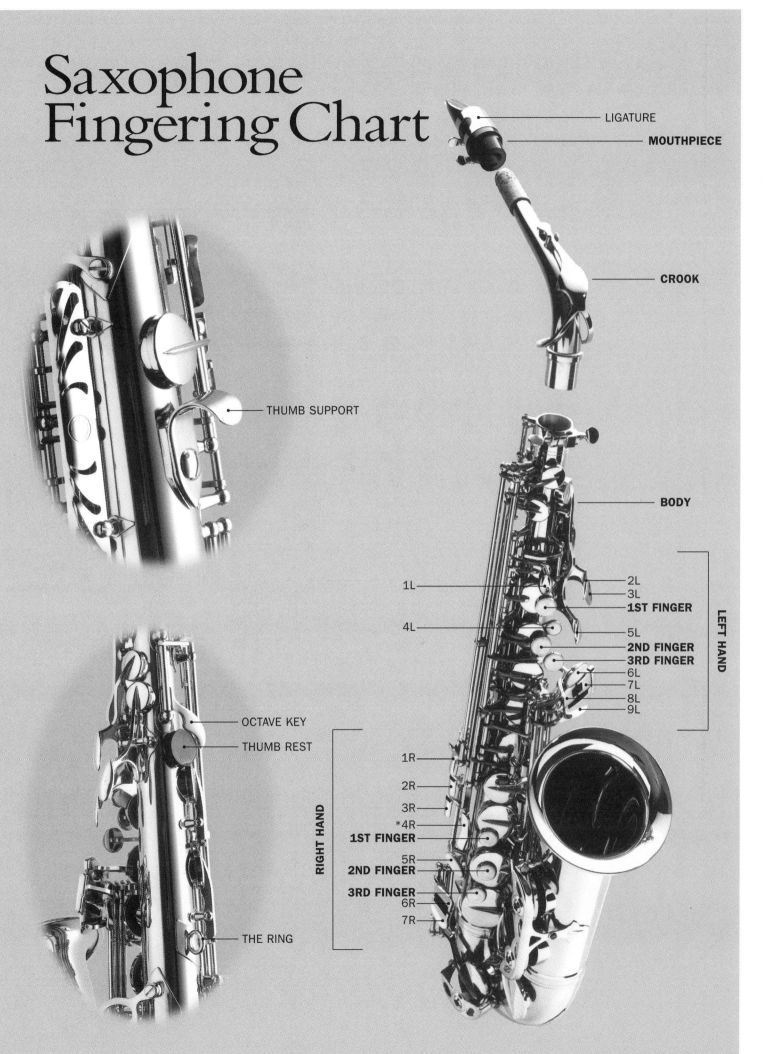

LIGATURE

MOUTHPIECE

CROOK

THUMB SUPPORT

BODY

OCTAVE KEY

THUMB REST

THE RING

1L
2L
3L
1ST FINGER
4L
5L
2ND FINGER
3RD FINGER
6L
7L
8L
9L

LEFT HAND

1R
2R
3R
*4R
1ST FINGER
5R
2ND FINGER
3RD FINGER
6R
7R

RIGHT HAND

* Not fitted on some saxophones

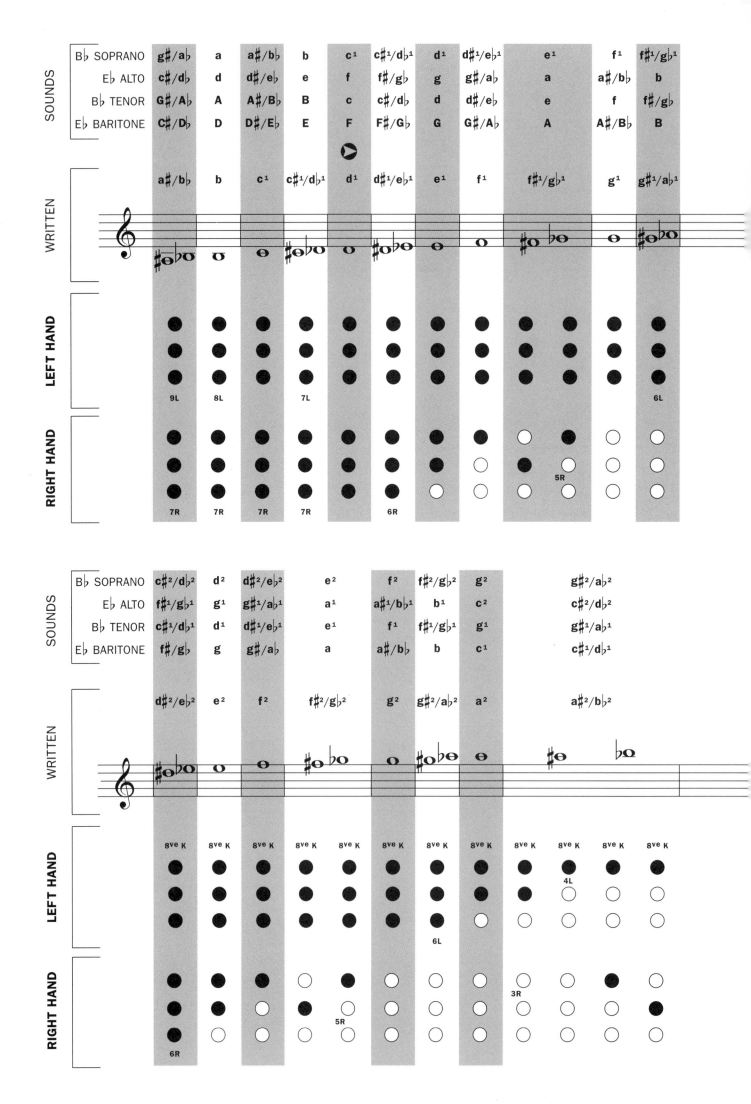

Indicates the lower limit of the best playing range

Indicates the upper limit of the best playing range

All Blues

Music by Miles Davis

All The Things You Are

Words by Oscar Hammerstein II
Music by Jerome Kern

Gentle up-tempo standard ♩ = c.180

p 'soft shoe' (*mf* more assertively on D.S.)

Solo I

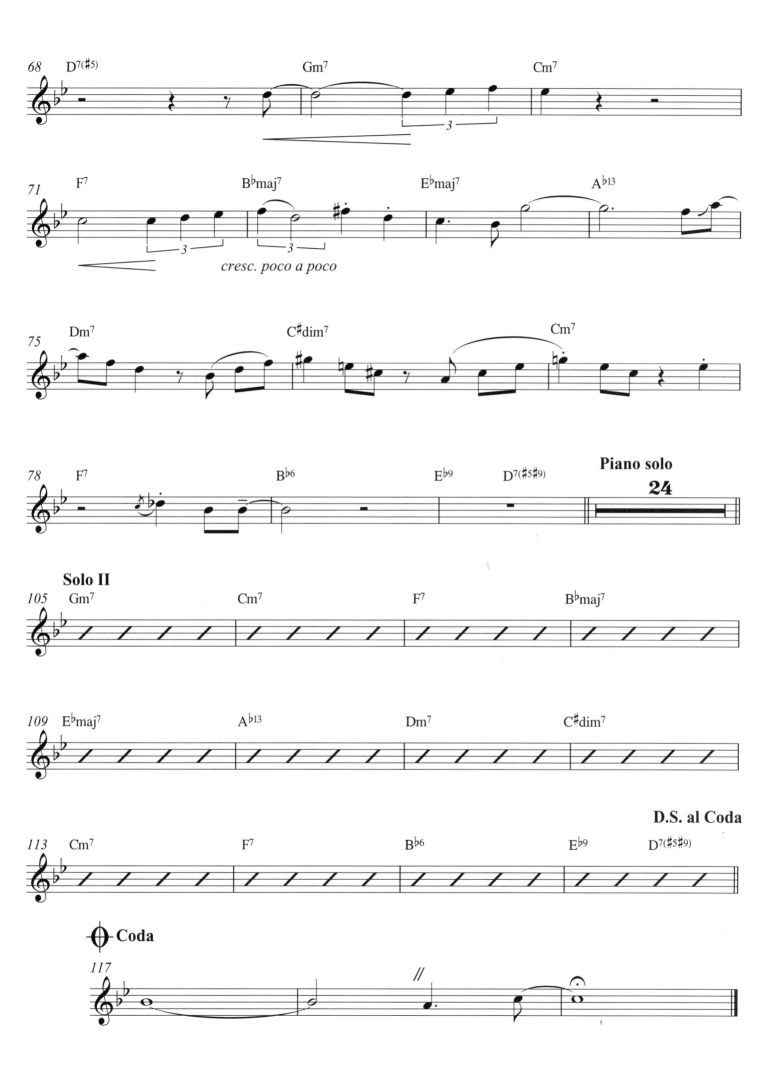

Corcovado (Quiet Nights Of Quiet Stars)

Words & Music by Antonio Carlos Jobim

Smooth latin ballad, with lazy 'late' feel

Freely at first

Tempo ♩ = c.64

In Walked Bud

Music by Thelonious Monk

Solo I

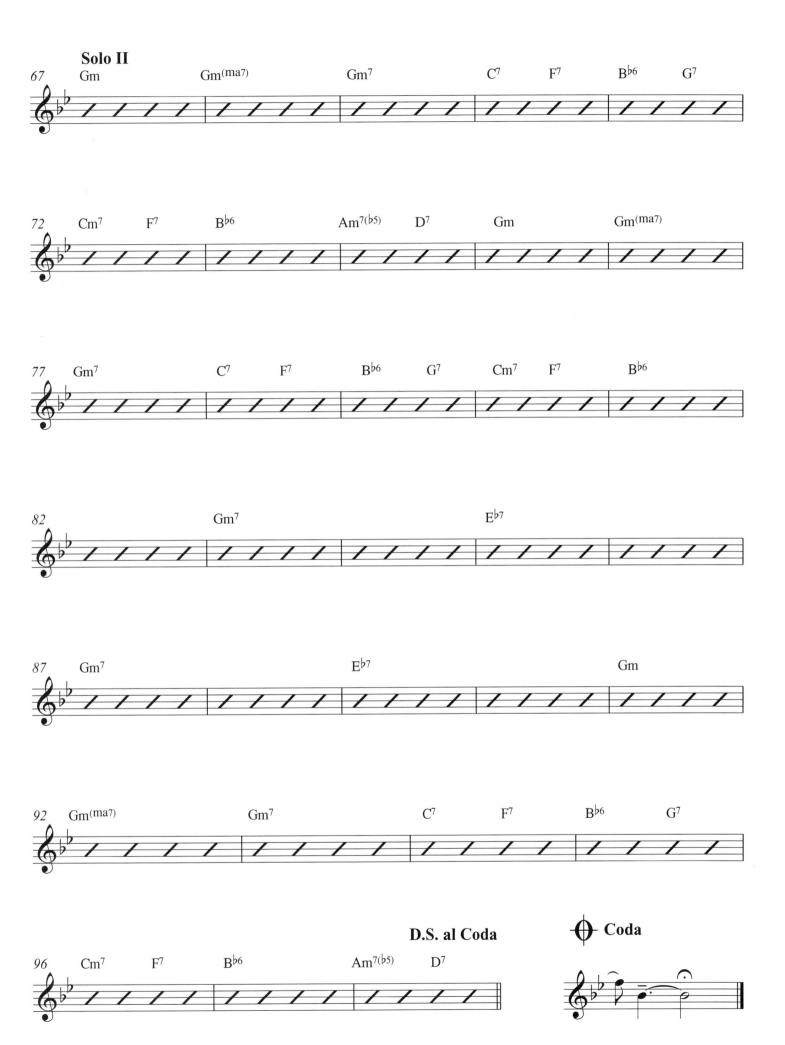

In A Sentimental Mood

Words & Music by Duke Ellington, Irving Mills & Manny Kurtz

Lullaby Of Birdland

Words by George David Weiss
Music by George Shearing

Solo I

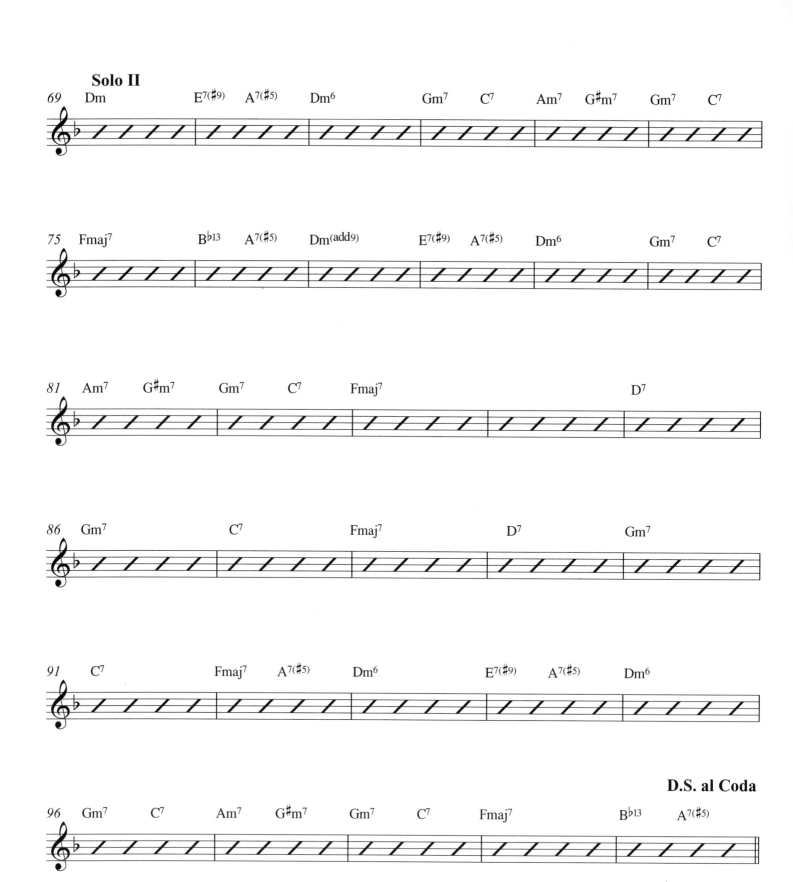

My Favourite Things

Words by Oscar Hammerstein II
Music by Richard Rodgers

Oleo

Music by Sonny Rollins

Cool bop-swing ♩ = 100

Count in

mf easy

(Piano solo)

to Coda

Solo I

The Sidewinder

Music by Lee Morgan

Cool Blue-beat, almost straight ♪s ♩ = 158

Bass cue:

The Way You Look Tonight

Words by Dorothy Fields
Music by Jerome Kern

Medium-fast bop ♩ = c.184

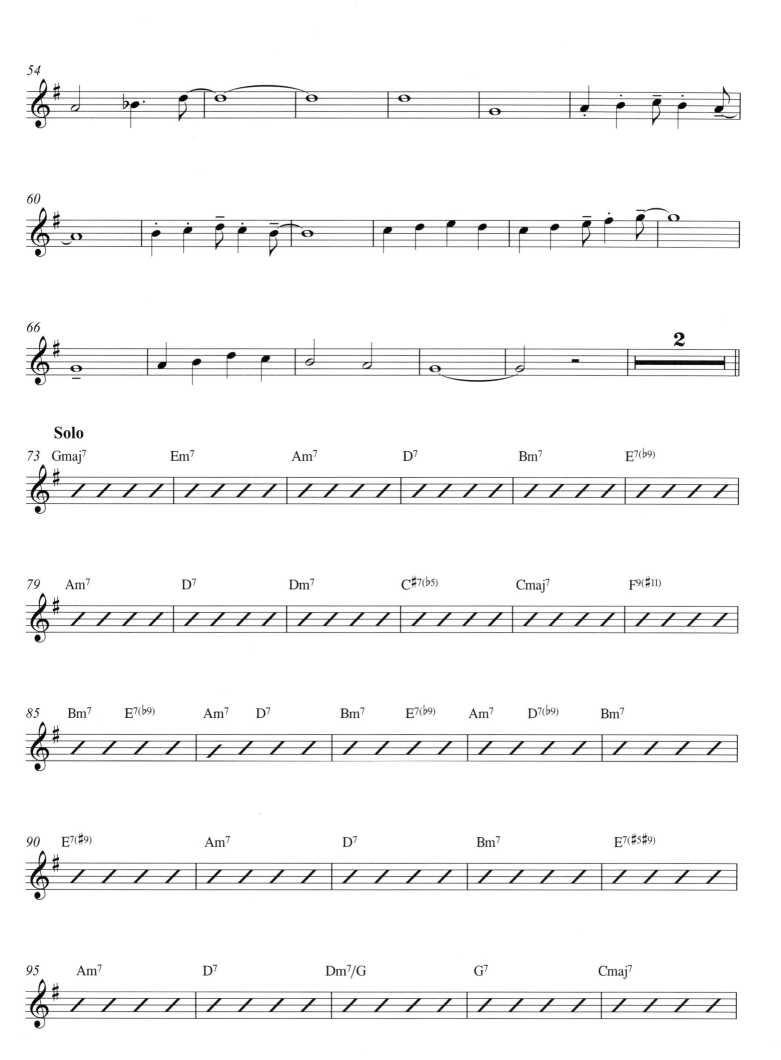

3 4 5 6 7 8 9

08/07 (63131)